Virginia Moffatt was born in London, one of eight children, some of whom are also writers. Her eldest brother has just published a book about theology, her eldest sister is a poet, and her twin sister a successful writer of commercial fiction.

Virginia has always wanted to write, but has only taken it seriously in the last decade. Since then she has studied for a diploma in Creative Writing at Oxford Department of Continuing Education, attended a Faber Academy weekend, a Guardian Masterclass weekend, and the York Festival of Writing. She has also completed one novel, *Echo Hall*, which she is submitting to agents, and the first draft of a second *The Wave* as part of Nanowrimo, which she is about to start editing.

Virginia has had stories published in several on-line magazines, *Evolve, Blankpages, One Million Stories*, and a couple of anthologies. She has co-written a play *Atos Stories* which was performed by Act Up! Theatre Company in 2013.

She lives in Oxford with her husband, Chris, and their three children.

Rapture
and
what
comes
after

Virginia Moffatt

GUMBO PRESS

Published by Gumbo Press

First Published 2014 by Gumbo Press
Printed using CreateSpace.

Gumbo Press
18 Caxton Avenue
Bitterne
Southampton
SO19 5LJ
www.gumbopress.co.uk

Rapture and what comes after, a selection of flash fiction first published on *A room of my own*, the blog of Virginia Moffatt.

A CIP Catalogue record for this book
is available from the British Library

ISBN 978-1500113834

for Chris, thanks for the rapture

contents

part one: rapture

part two: what comes after

part one: rapture

rapture

Sylvie wakes with a shiver. She can hardly feel her feet. Her back aches. She has slept with bent knees and now her right leg has cramps. She shakes it back to life, warming her toes as she does so. She doesn't mind the cold, not with Jim sleeping beside her and the knowledge of what today means. She turns towards the blissful sight of his face in the green tent light. She could gaze at his face for hours, but the sun will be rising soon, and they can't be late. She strokes his smooth skin and is rewarded with his eyes fluttering open and his lips reaching to kiss hers.

"It's time," she says.

This is the day they have been waiting for, since it was first predicted. At precisely six o'clock, on the 21st May, 2011, the sinners of the world will be swept away in earthquakes and storms, whilst the purest, the holiest will be carried up into heaven.

"At last." His grin is ecstatic.

They jump out of their sleeping bags, pulling their clothes on, eager to get moving.

"No time for breakfast," says Sylvie.

"We're not going to need any, where we're going."

He grabs her hands as they race towards the cliffs. The air is cool, the grey-blue sky lightening their way in preparation for the final dawn. Jim takes large strides up the stony path, forcing her to takes twice as many steps just to keep up. The exertion warms Sylvie; she soon forgets her aches and pains.

They arrive at the top, beaming at each other in breathless elation. At the edge of the cliff, they find a grey boulder. They sit against it, staring out across the sea at the horizon which is already lined with a strip of orange-gold. A seagull sweeps past and dives down into the waves below. Otherwise they are completely alone.

"I thought the others might come," she says, trying not to sound too disappointed.

"They were faint-hearted. Not true believers," he smiles at her. "It's better this way. Just us. You're the only one worth saving."

Oh the delight of hearing those words. After all this time, she still can't quite believe she is his chosen one. But here they are, just the two of them, right at the end. She snuggles against him, watching the clouds above the horizon turn pinky-orange. The wind has picked up causing the waves below to rise and fall, crashing against the rocks below. She looks at her watch, five to six. The sun will soon be here and then, and then...

"What will happen to the others do you think?"

"Earthquake, fire, pestilence, plague."

"Even my mother?"

This has always been her one reservation. Her mother isn't a believer, of course, but she is a harmless soul.

"I'm sorry sweetie, but your mother is one of the worst. She reads the Bible, but doesn't hear the message. It's right there in Genesis, and Matthew and Peter. This is the last day of tribulation, it's quite clear. Yet she doesn't believe it."

Jim has explained this before – the thousandth year since this, the seven thousandth since that. The importance of using the Hebrew and Gregorian calendars. If truth be told, Sylvie doesn't quite understand, but as Jim has always made clear, faith surpasses understanding. Besides, she always feels foolish if she questions him too much.

"I guess you're right."

"You know I am."

The sun is half way above the horizon, joined at the water's edge by its orange reflection, creating the momentary illusion that a ball of fire is burning the sea. It is getting warmer, despite the wind and the sky has paled into blue. A dog barks in the distance. Sylvie's watch says a minute to six. She squeezes Jim's hands. He squeezes back.

"I love you Sylvie," he says, and she trembles with joy. This is it. The two of them, about to be raised up to heaven. The sun pulls itself above the horizon blazing the sea with orange and red waves. They wait in eager anticipation. Any second now. The hands on Sylvie's watch march round to six. They wait patiently. Any second *now*.

They wait ... *any* second... and wait...The sun rises higher in the sky, fading into yellow; its reflection reduced to a tiny circle in the waves. Six-ten, six-twenty, six-thirty, seven. Nothing happens. *Nothing*. The sun keeps rising.

Sylvie's back is sore, her knees ache, her right leg is cramping. She is longing for a cup of tea and a fry up. But she doesn't dare to suggest it. How could Jim have got it wrong? He's always been so certain. Suddenly, Jim throws his hand against his forehead, as if he's heard her thought.

"Idiot. I'm a total idiot." He ruffles in his pocket and picks out a leaflet. "Look," he says, pointing to the date and the time. "I misread the time. It's six p.m. *not* a.m.."

Sylvie grins with delight.

"So, it's still going to happen then?"

"You betcha." He stands up and stretches. "Come on," he adds, "Breakfast. We'll come back later."

Hand in hand they run back across the cliffs. Towards the day ahead, and the rapture that is still to come

the scarf

Joe walks into the flat, throws his keys on the table, puts his feet up on the sofa, then pulls them off immediately. Lizzie may be gone but he can still hear her voice telling him not to get mud on the couch. He misses her already, wishing, not for the first time, that he had stopped her while he had the chance. He wishes that he wasn't so noble. That for once he'd been selfish and begged her not to go. Most of all he wishes he had sorted out plans for this evening. He should have invited Rick and Sam over, but now it's too late. They'll have been in the pub since six and will be at a level of drunken incoherence that is only fun if you're in at the beginning. Besides, waving Lizzie off was more exhausting then he had anticipated. He really isn't up to going out.

He stands and rifles through the DVDs on the shelf, not quite sure what he's in the mood for. *House* is too morose, *West Wing* too schmaltzy. At last he comes across his *Die Hard* collection. Lizzie not being a Bruce Willis fan, it must be two years since he last had a *Die Hard* bonanza. *Yippee-ki-yay motherfucker!* Tonight is *definitely* a *Die Hard* night. For the first time in two hours, he feels almost cheerful. He cooks a pizza, bringing it through with several beers, settling back on the couch prepared for non-stop action.

Soon he is so relaxed he is sprawled, shoes and all, along the length of the settee. By the time the film is over, the beige leather has scuff marks on it, and the floor is littered with empty beer cans. He's vaguely aware of the mess, but too drunk to care. It is only when he starts searching for the remote that reality pulls him back. It has slipped to the back of the couch. As he pulls it out, he dislodges a mass of red and purple material trapped behind the cushion: Lizzie's favourite scarf, the one he bought her for Christmas. He strokes the soft wool, folds his face into it, drinking in her lingering scent. Suddenly, her absence is all too present; even John McClane cannot help. *Die Hard 2* will have to wait till tomorrow.

He staggers into bed. Just as he is drifting off to sleep, the scarf clutched between his fingers, the horrible thought occurs to him. Perhaps she left it behind deliberately, a message to prepare him for the inevitable end to their relationship. Perhaps soon the scarf will be all he has left.

The plane taxis through the airport. Lizzie always hates this bit: the slow journey to the runway, the sudden increase in speed as they build momentum, the moment of take off that – despite all evidence to the contrary – she always imagines will end in a crash. She wishes Joe was with her, but Joe is long gone, left at the departure lounge to make his own way home, to the flat that she won't see for another year.

Not for the first time, she wonders why she is doing this, wonders what has possessed her to leave the man she loves for a freezing wasteland at the bottom of the earth. Scientific officer for the British Antarctic Survey might be the job she'd always dreamed of, but right now, she'd rather be at home with Joe.

She hates flying. She tries not to panic as she feels the

plane lurch forward, and the ground falls away below her. All she can do is close her eyes, grip the seat tight and picture Joe's face: his freckled nose, green eyes, the warmth of his smile. The plane rises and rises on steep incline that seems to last forever, until finally it reaches a steady plateau. As it levels off, her panic disappears; she opens her eyes.

Now they are safely in the sky, the earth a blaze of neon light below, she begins to relax. Now she can let the excitement of the adventure that she is embarking on flood through her body. A year in the Antarctic, learning to survive in the coldest, most inhospitable place on the planet. A job she has been aspiring to for the best part of a decade. Of course it's a wrench to leave Joe, but this is the chance of a lifetime, impossible to turn down. And lovely Joe hasn't stood in her way. It'll be tough being apart, but, she thinks, as the plane rises above the clouds, it can only make them stronger on her return.

Still she wishes she hadn't forgotten her scarf, the one Joe bought her for Christmas. She always wears it; it's like carrying a piece of Joe with her. She'll have to remember to ask for it, when she emails from Ascension Island. That way he can get it into the post, and there'll be a chance of it arriving before winter sets in. The stewardess comes by, offering refreshments, and films. She chooses both, smiling when she comes across *Die Hard* on the list. Normally, she wouldn't dream of watching it, but tonight, it is a way to bring Joe close. She slips on her headphones and loads the film.

Joe wakes at ten, with a dry throat and a hangover, the scarf still clutched in his hand. His phone is flashing. It's an email from Lizzie: *Currently holed up waiting for the plane to refuel. First flight so long and tedious I was forced to watch* Die Hard. *I can't believe I enjoyed it. Must be 'cos I'm missing you! Love you Lizziexxxx PS Please could you send my red and purple scarf? I think I left it on the sofa.*

Joe grins, the paranoia of the night before forgotten. If he's quick, he can reach the post office before it shuts.

night and day

Tick, tock, tick, tock, tick, tock.

Harriet wakes with a start from a sleep she hadn't meant to take. Her knees are stiff and her back is sore. The Roman numerals on the clock point to four-thirty already. The sun has reached the bottom of the hill, painting her sitting room wall red and orange. Funny how she used to hate that clock: the over-large gold leaves and the distorted cherubs seemed to sum up everything she disliked about her mother-in-law, Alison. How many afternoons had she and Paul sat in this very room, keeping Alison company, to that relentless tick, tock? Alison, whose days had ceased to please her, so she must destroy theirs, forcing them to stay and listen to her endless complaints: sciatica, rheumatism, loneliness. It was always such a relief when Paul's sister took over, and they were released to the night air, the moon, the stars, the dancing.

Tick, tock, tick, tock, tick, tock.

She's old, she needs me, Paul would say, as he whirled her across the dance floor like Fred Astaire. Though Harriet knew it was true, she didn't want him thinking that way too long. She'd pull him with her into the music, and soon, he was singing a different tune, telling her she was the one for him, night and day...She smiles at the memory. Time was, when her feet could glide to that tune and she could dance through to pink dawns and still feel fresh and ready for more. Such days they were, when her hair was black, and she could follow her desires so easily: when an hour with Paul seemed to last a thousand years. Now Alison is dead, Paul too, the children left home, and those days may as well have been a thousand years ago.

Tick, tock, tick, tock, tick, tock...

The rim of the sun is hanging on the horizon, sending shafts of red across the sky, making the moon blush. That clock has ticked its way through so many of her suns and moons in this house that she's come to love it for its ugliness. She even loved Alison a little in the end, as the years softened that sharp tongue and the arrival of grand-children brought some comfort. Now Harriet's own days are an uphill struggle, and walks are something to dread, she can understand the old woman somewhat better too. Still, it was more pleasant living here in the later years, once the kids were grown, when it was just her and Paul, and it was Sinatra's turn to sing, that she was the only one underneath the moon and sun... Those were the days when her hair was still dark, and he still thought her beautiful. Vanity of vanities - he wouldn't think her lovely now. *Tick, tock, tick,tock, tick, tock.*

Outside the shadows are falling. Night rushes across the garden, masking the signs of Spring; the almond tree beginning to blossom, the sparrows laying nests. She ought to get up and make herself a cup of tea, maybe ring Gill, who worries too much. Only last year she would have leapt up the minute she awoke, but her legs still feel shaky after her sleep, and she needs to catch her breath. There's no hurry after all. She might as well sit here for a while longer. She closes her eyes. Her breath shallows and a voice sings to her across the years... A voice that still thinks of her, wherever she is... She smiles, stretching out a hand for one last dance.

new year's resolution

The woman in the red dress is a nasty surprise. She stands at the doorway, the silk of the dress cut so perfectly it clings to the curves on her body like skin. It's lush, *she's* lush. Suddenly, the sexy outfit Suzy and I spent hours choosing feels tacky.

"Hi" she says, "You must be Kayleigh. Jack never stops talking about you."

Really? *Really?*

"Hi, and you are?"

"Alex, Jack's sister. Didn't he mention we shared a house?"

Dreams of a New Year kiss still intact, I totter into the small hallway.

I give her my coat, keeping the bolero jacket on. Suzy and I spent ages taping my boobs to the lime-green halter-neck I'm wearing, but I'm still a bit nervous of something going wrong. Alex waves me to the kitchen. Jack is standing with a group of friends, by a table of drinks and a big bowl of something resembling raspberry juice.

"Kayleigh! You came!" He gives me a hug. "Everybody, this is the woman who saves my life on a regular basis."

I try not to blush. This is *much* better. The group nod and smile, a couple introduce themselves as Dan and Rowan. A man I recognise from the office, says, "How come you get the sexy secretary?"

Jack smiles, "Hands off," and then to me, "Punch?" I slurp a drink that looks like raspberry juice, choking when I realise its strength. "Go easy on it – it's got quite a kick." I gulp it down to cover my confusion.

By nine o'clock I'm in the lounge dancing on the laminate floor. I feel loose with the music and the drink, sexy, ready for anything. It's only a matter of time before Jack finds me. Dan and Rowan are beside me shifting to the music with stiff, awkward movements. Rowan says she needs the loo and they leave. I take off my jacket, close my eyes and sway.

"Dance?"

It is the man from the kitchen. I'd rather it was Jack, but I don't know where Jack is, and I'm not sure how to say no. We gyrate together. I'm beginning to feel a little dizzy. It's nice dancing like this, but I don't want Jack getting the wrong idea. I make an excuse to run out to the kitchen where I plonk myself by the punchbowl and start telling jokes. There's not much punch left after an hour, but everyone is still laughing at me, so I must be funny, right? Someone turns the music off in the lounge. Jack enters. *Jack*. I gaze at him. He's so beautiful. Those brown eyes. The dimple on his chin. He wants me to follow him; *he wants me to follow him*.

"Come on," he says, "We're playing truth or dare."

In the living room someone spins a bottle. It points to Alex. She dares her friend to kiss a man with a ginger beard. To everyone's amusement they take their time about it. The bottle spins again, and again. People show a bit of flesh, kiss, share the odd secret. The bottle spins to Dan. He looks across at Rowan.

"Truth," he says, his voice sounding brittle. "Who

were you with last night?"

"Jools."

"Lying bitch," he walks out.

"I'm telling the truth." She's crying. Jack walks over and gives her a hug.

"Don't worry," he says. He's *so* kind. So lovely. Surely, it will be our turn soon?

The bottle spins to one of Jack's uni friends. He looks across at me

"Kayleigh. Show us your suspenders."

"You don't have to," says Jack. But everyone else is doing it. And I've got to the point I don't care. I stagger to the centre of the room, and hitch my skirt above the top of my stockings. There are catcalls and whistles and suddenly I feel as exposed as my suspenders. I turn round, tripping over someone's leg into Kitchen Man's lap.

"Thanks for dropping in" he says. He's not Jack, but now I am this close, I can't help noticing, his mouth has a hint of kissability. Still, it won't do to stay here. I pull myself up as fast as I can. Something tears. *Oh God no.* I'm doing a Janet Jackson right in front of Jack. Alex takes me upstairs to the bedroom, sorts out my top, and suggests I lie down.

"I'm fine. Honestly. I'm fine." It's not true, the room is moving round and round and my head is hurting. "Jack...".

"Don't worry. I'll explain." She switches off the light, leaving me alone in the dizzy darkness.

When I look at the clock again it is nearly midnight. I've got to get up. I heave myself off the bed. My hair is all over the place, but I can't find a brush. I feel sick. I've got to find Jack before midnight. I've *got* to.

Downstairs the lounge is crowded. *5,4,3,2,1: Happy New Year!*. There is a cheer. People snog. Poppers go off. Outside fireworks explode. Where's Jack? I push my way out into the hall. The kitchen is empty, but the back door is open. I can see two people standing by the fence. They have the look of long-term lovers. The man turns round as I come out into the garden. Suddenly I am stone cold sober. It's *Jack*. Jack. And the woman? It's bloody Rowan. Dan was right. She *is* a lying bitch.

I run back inside, resolving then and then to give up men for good.

My New Year's resolution lasts for less than a minute. As I'm looking for my jacket, I run into Kitchen Man.

"Hey Kayleigh. How about a New Year kiss?" He pulls me towards him. The feeling of his tongue in my mouth is not unpleasant. He's not Jack, but then again Jack is not the man I thought he was. Perhaps that works in reverse. And it does seem a shame to waste the suspenders.

I move into Kitchen Man's body and kiss him back.

househunting

It was Dwayne's idea to look for somewhere bigger. Ever since Marcia had moved in, sprawling her possessions across the flat, with a casualness that had soon passed from endearing to aggravating, he'd found himself feeling increasingly pressed for space. It was wonderful having her in the flat – he still couldn't believe it when he woke up to find her besides him – it was just he hadn't anticipated she'd bring *quite* so much stuff with her. That her books and CDs, shoes and handbags, would spread through the tiny flat like tsunami, scattering his precious possessions – Marvel comics, CDs and computer games – in its wake.

At first he was pleased that Marcia responded so enthusiastically; but, now, after a month of bombardments from estate agents, and weekends of non-stop viewings, he was beginning to wish he'd never suggested it in the first place. Particularly since his preference – a large airy flat in a block in the city centre with an on-site gym – seemed to have been swept aside in the endless search for the perfect house in the perfect neighbourhood. And judging by the nature of those up-market multi-cultural neighbourhoods, full of parks, shops and schools, it seemed that Marcia was already making plans for a time when they would be more than just a couple.

He adored Marcia, he really did. She made him happier than any woman ever had done in the past. He couldn't imagine life without her now. And yet, he found it difficult to plan for even a week ahead. A future full of nappies was beyond his comprehension. He'd been trying to tell her this for days, but somehow, there never seemed to be enough time; particularly since every conversation seemed to be reduced to the pros and cons of the property they had just visited.

Now, as they were greeted by the owner of a promising-looking three bedroom terrace in an approved part of town, Dwayne's worst nightmare presented itself. The man, who was called Gary, had a baby on his shoulder, another child clinging to his legs, and two more in the corridor. They were screeching with delight at the prospect of visitors. Harassed didn't begin to describe the look on the man's face. Marcia, of course, was undeterred. She bounced across the doorstep shaking Gary's hand, full of raptures about the house, the children, the neighbourhood.

Dwayne followed in her wake, immediately prepared to dislike a home that was so filled with noise and clutter. And yet, despite the toys scattered from the toy-box all over the living room floor, despite the wails of the baby, and its three older siblings who followed them from room to room full of squeals and chatter, despite Gary's obvious stress, he couldn't help thinking this really was a lovely place to live.

The lounge diner had been stripped down to polished bare floors, the original fireplace decorated with tiles depicting delicate red roses. The extended kitchen with its skylight ensuring the room was bright and airy. The enclosed garden with its decking and barbecue. In spite of himself, he could picture dining with Marcia in that kitchen, the pair of them making love in the lounge afterwards, as fire crackled in the grate. He glanced at Marcia as she picked her way over some broken bits of Lego, and saw from her smile she'd had the same thought.

Climbing the stairs proved more challenging. The children seemed to be everywhere, playing a complicated game of mountain climbing, whilst their father, bringing up the rear, somewhat feebly entreated them to take care. Dwayne was grateful when they reached the landing, and rushed off into their bedrooms, leaving the grown-ups to explore at their leisure.

The main bedroom was exactly what they had been looking for. There was plenty of space: built-in shelves which should absorb all Marcia's books, and large enough wardrobes for clothes and shoes. The second toy-strewn room was smaller, but would make a perfect guest room. Whilst the final room, furnished with a cot and tiny bed, would be perfect for his comic collection.

Marcia flashed him a grin as she popped to the toilet; despite himself he was hooked, and she knew it. It was when he reached the last room that things became awkward. He was peeking out at the garden when one of the children managed to get stuck in the toy box. He burst out into a loud wail that his siblings could not assuage.

"Do you mind?" said the father, handing him the perplexing baby, as he hurried to comfort the child.

Dwayne had no option but to take the bundle of flesh and hold it gingerly on his shoulder as he watched the other man do. Babies terrified him. He had never even picked one up. To his surprise, its warm body was less fragile than he'd imagined. And instead of smelling of nappies, its odour was sweet and milky. Equally surprising was the sudden rush of protectiveness he felt towards the tiny creature he was cradling on his chest. As Marcia walked back in the room, smiling at his unusual pose, he was surprised at how comfortable he felt. When Gary returned, he found himself giving the baby back with some reluctance, almost envying the other man as the child nestled on his shoulder. He might have stood their indefinitely if Marcia's nudge hadn't reminded him it was time to go. There were another three houses to visit, and though he suspected, like him, she had already made up her mind, she would want to see them just to be sure.

They left the house, and climbed into the car. Marcia was looking at her phone, plotting the route ahead, as always. And it came to him, then, that perhaps he'd misjudged her. Perhaps she already knew him better than he knew himself. Now he had seen the future he realised she might be right; perhaps it wouldn't be so bad after all.

submission

The Europeans arrived after prayer-time. Khadija and I were mopping the tiles in the courtyard. We watched them climb the stairs. They were tired and didn't see us.

"Look at her clothes," I cried, "She is practically naked!"

"That's what the Western girls wear," said Khadija, who'd grown up in the hotel and was used to their funny ways. "The small trousers are called "shorts". The top, is a "T" shirt. They wear them to be cool."

This was odd. When I want to be cool, I wear loose clothing. In the middle of the day, I rest. I couldn't imagine why the woman wanted everyone to see her long tanned limbs, the curve of her breasts.

"How can her hair be so yellow?" I asked.

"Hair dye probably." I pulled a puzzled look. "Like henna. We colour our hands, they colour their hair."

How strange, I thought. But I was having to get used to strange things since my marriage to Bilal. Since leaving my village and living with his people. In a hotel, you see all sorts. Soldiers on leave from their garrisons. Guides preparing to take the tourists to the desert. Business men on their way to a conference in the resorts. Khadija said we'd have our fair share of Europeans in the summer, but it was spring, and these two had caught me unawares. I supposed I'd get used to their peculiarities, but it wouldn't be easy. I continued to wash the floor.

At supper time, I brought Bilal his evening meal. When

his Father is away, he's the only one able to manage the front desk. He can read, write, speak French, do Arithmetic. Sometimes he is there for hours on end. One day, when Bilal has taught me everything he knows, I will be able to take my turn. But that is in the future, bringing him food is all I can do to help for now.

When I reached the desk, I found my husband in a fury; the man had tried to bargain for a cheaper room. How dare he? We offer the best prices in town. Everyone knows. That's why the foreigners come, because we're cheap and safe. Yet, here was this ignorant fool acting like he was in the souk. We shrugged at the mysterious ways of Westerners and I made my way back across the courtyard, passing the couple as I did so. I did not meet their eyes, but I was aware of the woman looking at me with distaste. I marvelled at her ignorance.

Later, in bed, I asked Bilal, "Why does she wear such clothes?"

"Who knows? Perhaps, she thinks it brings her freedom."

What freedom? I wondered. It seemed to me that she was lost, in need of guidance. But I had no idea how I could offer her that. We didn't even speak the same language. Presently, Bilal drew me to him, and we forgot the strangers upstairs. It was a hot night, but I slept well.

We woke as usual to the muezzin's call. We rose, prayed, and went about our daily business - Bilal to the front desk, Khadija and I to the cleaning. As always I started my day praising Allah for finding me a husband like Bilal, and a family that welcomes me. Bilal's parents treat me like their daughter; Khadija is my soul-sister; and he is so tender, so kind. Sometimes he suggests I should abandon my hijab, like a modern Moroccan. But that's because he studied in Casablanca for a while, and was caught by city ways. I am happy to cover up, I say, to submit to Allah's will. It is fitting not to parade my beauty in public. The avoidance of vanity seems to me the true practice of Islam. He tries to argue, and then, seeing my determination, laughs and kisses me instead. Truly, I have all the luck.

I am not so sure of this European woman. Yesterday she and her friend rose late. They asked Bilal about hiring a Grands Taxi to go to the desert and he directed them to the market square. They packed their bags and departed, we thought for good. But a few hours later, they returned to check in for another night. They were red faced, and stiff with each other. That night we heard shouting from their room. Bilal said money was mentioned but that was all he could translate. They left for good this morning. Yusuf told us that he saw them take the bus back to Marrakech, they were barely speaking. Khadija and I are still wondering what they were arguing about.

Later, when I cleared the room, I found a bottle marked "Garnier Nutrisse. Light Ash Blonde." The words meant nothing to me. I threw it away.

white wedding

"Hello." His voice is rough, grizzled from sleep. I should have called a bit later; I know how he loves his Saturday morning lie-ins.

"Dan - it's me, Jen."

"Hey little sis, how are you?"

"Fine. Actually, more than fine. I've got some news. Or should say, we've got some news. Ruth and I."

"Oh?" Dan sounds a little uncertain, as he often is when I mention Ruth's name. But he's my brother, and I love him, so I plough on.

"We're getting married."

"What?"

"We're getting married. Going for the works, white wedding, big cake and a party. We want a *big* party. And I want you to give me away."

"What?"

"Ruth's got her parents, I don't. I have you. I want you to do it." There is silence at the end of the phone. "Dan?" Still silence. Then: "People like you don't get married."

"What's that supposed to mean?"

"Lesbians, gays, whatever the correct term is these days." His venom is startling. I thought we'd got over this.

"Dan!"

"Don't get me wrong Jen, I'm happy for you. I really am. Ruth's nice enough. I can see she makes you happy..." I say nothing. He continues, now he has started, it's clear he wants to get this off his chest. "It's not right, though is it? Two women marrying each other. Marriage is for a man and a woman. It just doesn't make sense otherwise."

I think of marshalling some arguments. About Equality. Justice. Love. But I can sense he is only just getting going. I don't think I can bear it. So I hang up the phone and return to the living room where Ruth is Ruth, wise, compassionate, kind. But even she cannot alleviate this hurt. Not now, anyway. Dan is my only brother; his kids, my only family. If they turn their backs on me, what will I become? I cannot explain this to Ruth entirely, Ruth who is so central to her parents and siblings, so loved, so accepted. She does her best, but she's never known what this feels like: to be outside the fold, excluded from the love you believed would last. I thought Dan had got over this. Clearly, I was wrong.

But, after a long run, through the puddled park, the yellow-orange leaves drifting about me like blossom, and a hot bath filled with rose-scented bubbles, I feel better. Sod Dan. Sod him. Ruth and I are getting married. The day we never thought possible is going to be ours. I set about planning with a vengeance.

Finn wakes me at six. He's off on a school trip but he's seen about the wedding on Facebook.

"I spoke to Dad. He's a tool, Auntie Jen. A total tool."

"I'd say respect your father, but on this issue..."

"I'll give you away." My eyes prick with tears.

"Won't you get in trouble with your Dad?"

"I won't tell if you won't." That makes me smile.

Finn's rebellious streak has always reminded me of my own teenage naughtiness.

"You're on."

"I know it's cheesy, but I do love a white wedding."

"Who was that?" asks Ruth, sleepily as I hang up. I explain. "Thank God for the youth of today," she says, and we drift back to sleep.

The weeks before the wedding pass in a flurry of activity. Dan calls occasionally to see how I am. He never mentions the wedding, or Finn's participation, and I don't push it. I'm hoping that once the deed is done, we can return to our uneasy truce.

Nonetheless, on the day of the wedding, I can't help feeling disappointed when Finn turns up alone.

"Auntie Jen, you look gorgeous." He gives me a kiss.

"So do you." The little boy I once babysat has become, in top hat and tails, a handsome young man.

"How are you feeling?" he asks.

"Nervous, happy, excited." I don't say that I wish his dad was here. It's brilliant he's stepped up for me, but I wish he was Dan. "Thanks for being here."

He squeezes my arm, "My pleasure," and then looking at his watch, "Shall we?" We walk out to the waiting White Bentley, decorated with white ribbon, a bouquet of pink roses in the back. I am off to marry the woman I love - nothing else matters.

The journey is short. We pull up outside the front of the red-brick hotel. The sun is glowing yellow in a bright blue sky. It's a perfect day for it. We walk into the hallway, where Ruth is standing with her parents. I catch my breath. This is the first time I've seen her in her dress:

it is a simple white silk that hugs are willowy figure and brings out the colour in her cheeks. She looks stunning. I blow her a kiss. She blows one back. The guests are already seated, and now it is time for Ruth to walk down the aisle ahead of me. I watch her glide to the front, conscious of how lucky I am. I am about to start my own walk with Finn, when someone taps me on the shoulder.

"Hey, little sister," It is Dan. Unbelievably, it is Dan. "My job I think," he says to Finn. I am about to protest, but Finn just grins and says, "Go for it." Dan takes my arm.

"Sorry. I've been a plonker."

"You have."

"Start again?" I look up at my big brother, seeing the sincerity of his apology in his eyes. I look down the aisle where Ruth is waiting for me with the biggest smile on her face. I nod. It's a nice day for it, after all.

happy birthday, darling

It always makes me happy to find you a present I know you'll love, and the one before me is a real beauty. A rare Dresden Shepherdess statue - she stands holding a bouquet, raising her floral skirt, and smiling, one presumes, at a lover approaching her. I am always buying you such gifts, but this one is a little special. It has taken me years to track her down, and I have finally done it, just in time for your fiftieth.

As ever, when I begin to wrap, I am reminded of the moment I first saw you: standing at the bottom of the steps to your flat, sobbing on your boyfriend's shoulder. You didn't see me, of course. For this was in the period before we knew each other, in the days before love surprised us. At that time, I was just a stranger hovering on the periphery of your distress.

I wasn't even living in the neighbourhood, just passing through on my lunch break, when I happened to witness the removal man lose his footing on the top step, letting slip a large brown box as he righted himself. It bounced to the ground too quickly for anyone to stop it, bursting open on the pavement, spilling its contents - your grandmother's collection of Dresden Shepherdesses - across the pavement, where they crashed and shattered into thousands of pieces. I am not usually interested in other people's dramas, but there was something about your fragile despair that affected me: the droop of your shoulders, the strands of black hair falling in front of your eyes, the depth of your weeping. It was enough to make me resent the man who was comforting you, enough to make me wish that I could be the one to wrest away that tearful smile, encouraging you whilst you cleared up the mess. I watched until my stomach rumbled, reminding me that my lunch was nearly over, and it was none of my business anyway.

It was two years before we met properly. Two years in which your relationship with - I always want to call him Geoffrey, but wasn't it actually Tim? - fell apart as spectacularly as that box on the stairs. Two years in which I managed client's accounts, moved from one unsatis-factory house-share to another, and looked for an impossible woman like you. Eventually, sick of arguments about kitchen rotas, I invested my savings in a tiny studio flat three streets away from you. I had no idea you were still living in the area, no hope that I might ever meet you, and then suddenly there you were. Miracles don't happen to people like me, but there you were sitting in my downstairs neighbour's living room when I popped down to borrow some milk, and I was dragged in, somewhat reluctantly, for an introductory cup of tea. I am not the most social of people, but nor do I find it easy to refuse someone as effusive as George. I stepped across the doorway, my reluctance disappearing when I saw you on the couch. At first, I was my usual tongue tied self, until the conversation turned to moving days; you described the horror of the dropped box, the broken Dresden shepherdesses, and I found my opening. Thanks to you - your charm, your grace, your way of putting people at ease - our relationship was able to progress. You made it seem so easy, were so grateful that I wasn't Tim, or

Geoffrey (you had several boyfriends before me, I always muddle them up), that I was swept along and before we knew it I was proposing to you on the eve of the Millenium.

We've had our struggles since but we've been happy, haven't we darling? I know we regret the lack of children - those miscarriages hurt us both - but we have not let them blight our lives. And being childless allows us to maintain a lifestyle that is the envy of our friends (Two foreign holidays a year in these austerity stricken times is good going by anyone's standards). I know sometimes it frustrates you that I find it hard to express my feelings for you, to tell you how much I love you, how grateful I am that you are in my life. I am a quiet man by nature; words don't come easily to me. But I know you understand that this is who I am, and love me anyway. You recognise that my gifts express my love for you, in a way my words cannot.

For fifteen years, I have been buying you statues, helping you recreate the beloved collection you lost all those years ago. This final one - now completely covered in wrapping paper - will be the crowning glory. I cannot tell you how much pleasure it will give me to see you unwrap it tomorrow.

I place it in the cupboard ready for the morning; stopping to look at the picture of you by my side of the bed. *Happy Birthday, darling.* I kiss you before I walk down the stairs. In love, sometimes, actions speak louder than words.

let it snow

The snow is beginning to fall in light flakes as he leaves the house. He hates to leave her. He'd much prefer to stay inside, lying by the log fire, listening to Christmas songs, drinking red wine. But he's due at the conference this evening and he has lingered longer than he should. He must get moving if he is to stay ahead of the weather. Though it is only half past three, the sun has long been smothered by the grey clouds dominating the sky. The air is cold and damp; his feet are already dusted with white powder. At the gate, he turns to see her standing in the doorway, radiant in the glow of the hall light. She blows him a kiss, "Safe journey," she calls. He raises his arm in farewell, walks to the car, revs the engine, and watches in the mirror as her cottage passes from his sight.

She stands on the front step, watching his blue Renault accelerate down the road. She wishes he'd been able to stay. What kind of conference starts on a Sunday night anyway? It will be five days till she will see him again. Five days! They have Skype and instant messaging, but it's never the same. She wants him here by her fireside, gazing at the delightful flames licking the logs, sipping wine while Michael Bublé serenades them.

Still there's no point shivering on the doorstep. She closes the door, shutting out the frightful weather, returning to the living room, where she begins the dreary task of tidying up the remnants of their lazy afternoon. Tea cups, and empty chocolate wrappers, the sections of the *Observer* spread across the room. How could two people make so much mess? By the time she has cleared away and put the laundry on, it is nearly four o'clock. Outside, the snow is falling faster in thick globules. It is hard not to worry a little, watching the darkening sky, but it'll be at least another hour before he arrives at his destination. What she needs is a movie to distract her till then. She settles in front of *Love Actually*. If she can't have the real thing, movie love will do.

The traffic is clear for the first few miles. People round here are wise enough to stay put on a day like this. He tries to ignore the feelings of regret, as he accelerates towards the road that will take him to the motorway. But there's no point regretting what he can't have. As he reaches the A road, the sky is darkening from grey to black.

He puts his windscreen wipers onto full speed. They creak as they move back and forth across the window cleaning off the snow that is replaced as quickly as it disappears. He slows down to fifty. No point taking risks in this weather. To distract him from thoughts of frozen cars and pile ups, he switches the radio on, smiling ruefully as it blares out Sinatra singing *Let it Snow*. He wishes he could brush the weather off quite so easily, particularly as the road sign flashes delays ahead. In the distance he can see red tail lights, blurring through the falling snow and ice, crawling slowly up the hill. He turns the heater up as he approaches the queue, his speed reducing to thirty, twenty, ten miles an hour. This journey is going to be longer than anticipated.

The film comes to an end in a welter of feel-good moments that make her feel warm, until she realises it is nearly six and she hasn't heard from him. There's no point panicking, she tells herself, as she moves to the kitchen to heat up some soup. Conditions are bad out there, he'll ring soon and she'll be able to relax. She watches as little red bubbles appear on the surface of the soup. Outside, the snow is piling up in the garden. If it carries on much longer, the road out of the village will be impassable.

It's happened before – last time for three days – and of course she managed. But it would be so much more pleasant if he was with her. Just as she is pouring the soup into a bowl, and buttering a crisp slice of baguette, her phone bleeps, an answer to her unspoken prayer. *M6 closed. Heading back.* She eats her soup, grinning at the thought that before too long, he'll be sauntering back up her path. That she'll have at least tonight and with any luck, tomorrow as well.

Once he has made the decision to return, he feels light headed. He has never missed a sales conference before. But if work kick up, he can always cite the policeman telling him it was too dangerous to continue. He resists the urge to drive fast, and it takes another hour to reach the outskirts of her village. In the time he has been driving, the lane has become clogged with slow. He pushes through inch, by inch, as he creeps back to her. He reaches the final bend, and the steep descent towards her home. Now he is driving so slowly, it feels like he is barely moving. He is desperate to arrive, but she has told him before of snow casualties on this road; he doesn't intend to be one.

At last he is here. He parks outside the spot he left five hours before. He is covered in snow before he even reaches the step, but he doesn't care. Within seconds, the door is open, and she is there, in the warm glow of the hall light. She drags him, closing the door behind him, shutting out the frightful night.

It will be snowing for some time to come. Let it.

Have I told you about her?

Have I told you about her yet? I hope you don't mind me going on like this. The truth is, I can't stop thinking about her. I've never met anyone like her. Never. I still can't believe she's even looked at me twice. But she has. And we've been together six weeks already. I've never been happier.

Have I told you about the way her hair falls? Usually, she wears it up, in a twisted bun, or a plait, or a ponytail. But when she lets it down, the curls flow down her back and over her shoulder, sparking gold in the sunlight. I want to bury my head in that mass of curls, let my fingers run through her astonishing silky tresses.

Have I told you about her honey skin? How on these summer days, we lie in the park, lightly clothed, her head resting on my chest. I stroke her bare arms, kiss the nape of her neck, shiver with delight at the warmth of her body pressed so close to mine. I have never felt so alive, so real, so free.

Have I told you how clever she is? At dinner time (in my flat or hers, as long as I'm with her, I don't care which) I could listen to her talk for hours. She knows about history and literature and politics. She talks of scientific discoveries that I've never heard of, countries, I've never been to. She holds me in the palm of her hand.

Have I told you about her kindness? That she visits her aging grandmother once a week to do the shopping.

How, when we are in the street, she will stop to help a random stranger, just because they've lost their way, or their dog. And how quickly she soothes all my work upsets away.

I'm sorry to keep going on like this - it's just I've never felt this way about anyone before. But, have I told you? Have I told you? Have I told you? I'm the happiest man alive.

no doubt about it

"Pete's asked me to move in."

"Fantastic news!" Jenny beams back at Jack, and then, seeing the uncertainty in his eyes, "...isn't it?"

"I think so..."

"But?"

"I'm not sure I'm sure enough. If you know what I mean?"

Jenny bursts out laughing. "You silly clot. You're perfect for each other. You share the same political views, had similar upbringings, complement each other's personalities. You even finish each other's sentences. You're an old married couple already, this will just seal the deal."

"You think so?"

"I know so. Take it from one who knows you - I've never seen you this happy."

Her words are reassuring, but, when Jack leaves her to cycle home by the canal, the doubts begin to creep in again. Loving is always fun with Pete, but living together? Jack likes his freedom. He likes cycling in the sunshine, watching the narrow boats meander along the waterway, with no cares in the world, and no-one to tell him he's late home for dinner. He likes the thought that tomorrow, if he so wished, he could jack in his job, take his life-savings and hitch around the world. He likes the anticipation of meeting Pete at the end of a busy day. But living with him? That's entirely different.

He reaches the flat, grabs a bite to eat, puts on his uniform, and cycles to work, grateful for a busy late shift that avoids him having to think too much. It is not until seven that things begin to settle down, and he has time to catch up on his notes. He has been sitting at the nurses' station for about twenty minutes, when he is aware of someone hovering besides him.

"Excuse me," the elderly man says, "Sorry to bother you, but could you please check my wife's drip? I'm not sure it is attached properly."

Jack is happy to oblige; he always prefers interaction with patients to paperwork. He fixes the drip, leaving the couple together, touched by how solicitous the man is with his wife; checking her feet are not in pain, puffing her pillows up, fetching her cardigan. He returns to his computer. At eight thirty, as visiting hours come to an end, he is conscious he hasn't seen the old man leave. When he walks back to the bay, he finds the old man sitting in his seat, holding his wife's hand. She is sleeping peacefully.

"Beautiful, isn't she?" the old man says. Jack nods. "I'm sorry, is it time to go now?"

"Yes."

"I hate this bit. Forty years married, and not a night apart till this illness." He pulls himself up from the seat, kisses his wife on the forehead, picks up his coat and walks back up the ward. "Are you married yourself?" Jack shakes his head. "You should be. Best thing in the world."

"Really? Doesn't it get...boring after a while?"

"Not when you're with the right person. It's never

boring with the right person." They reach the nurses' station. "I'll see you tomorrow maybe?" Jack nods again and watches him shuffle out of the ward. He thinks of the wife left sleeping, secure in her husband's love. He thinks of the old man, taking the long bus journey home alone. He wonders if Pete and he will last that long. And then, as if in answer to his thought, his phone flashes, it's Pete. *Got an answer for me yet?* And suddenly, he realises he is sure. There is no doubt about it. No doubt at all. *Yes, and YES!* He texts back. He looks at the clock, an hour left to go. After work, he will cycle round to Pete's and tell him to his face.

a woman's work

I wake at six to an unfamiliar ceiling. Alex is snoring, and I can just hear the sounds of Ben stirring next door. So I must be in the right place. It takes a moment for realisation to dawn with the sunlight peeking through the cracks in the curtain. We won, though I never thought we would. We Won. Therefore We Moved. And now my life will change in – oh, so many ways.

I don't need to stagger out of bed, and peek out of that curtain, to know the street below will be full of paparazzi. I've no intention of doing *that* – giving them the chance of a rapid snap. Me in my nightie with my hair all over the place. No doubt the day will come and I'll let down my guard. Some photographer will get lucky on the back of my hitched up skirt or drunken pratfall. But not today.

Cherie, Sarah, Sam. They've all been here before me. Modern women – who juggled careers and children and lived lives independent from their husbands – until they reached this bedroom. How did they stand it? Cherie, one of the brightest of her generation, reduced in the public eye to a scrounging scally. Didn't Sarah have a job in PR once? Somehow it submerged into Twitter and her husband's smelly socks. As for Sam, she gave it all up the minute she crossed the threshold. A family can only take one alpha parent after all. And someone has to be at home for the kids.

Of course I supported Alex when he said he wanted to

be party leader. A girl wants to stand by her man when she thinks he's in with a chance. I just didn't expect him to get it. I consoled myself with the thought it wouldn't last too long, that we'd return to obscurity soon. Until the Prime Minister surprised us all with a snap election, that is. Even that should have been a shoo-in. Our electoral pain should have been over in a month. We should have lost with dignity, and got on with the rest of our lives, knowing that at least we tried.

All it took was a few thousand votes. A two per cent swing the other way and we'd have been back at home drowning our sorrows. Because of those few thousand people bothering to go to the ballot box, I'm lying here staring at an unfamiliar ceiling, wondering how the hell we can manage a life that had enough complexity in it already.

The clock blinks six-fifteen in red digitalised numbers. Ben potters into the room and climbs into the bed for an early morning cuddle. Alex continues to snore. In a minute, Alice will wake. In a minute, I'll have to work out where we have breakfast, find uniforms, determine how we get the children to school. In a minute Alex will be woken and dragged off into a world that will consume him utterly. I doubt that I will see him much before bed time. As for me? I'll do what I always do, sort out the kids, and stand by my man. Maybe it's subservient, maybe I'm letting the sisterhood down, but right now I can't see what else to do. A woman's work is never done.

one last kiss

One last kiss, but it really has to be the last. I hate to leave you, but I have to go. I suppose one more won't hurt. And another, and another. Now I really must go. I must pull myself, reluctantly, from your arms and say goodbye. For I am already late for work. And yet, the taste of you, the look of you, the touch of you... It is hard to prise myself away, particularly with a kiss like that. But prise I must, if I am to catch the bus that will get me to the office by ten. You tempt me with one more, and another, and another. Till at last we manage to drag ourselves apart from our final kiss. A kiss so intense it has the power to propel me from the house, racing down the street, with a smile on my face so broad, it even cheers the grumpy bus driver.

The bus jerks around the corner, throwing me onto my seat. I switch on my iPod, listening to Justin Timberlake singing our song, over and over again. My fingers tap texts, responding to your instant replies, connecting us even as I am driven further away from you. Though once I am at the office, I have to be more circumspect. My desk is right in front of the boss who believes he has my undivided attention for the next eight hours.

It is hard to use my phone often, in such circumstances, but he cannot read my mind. He cannot stop me thinking of you. All the while I am translating his tiny scrunched up writing into clean, typed prose on the screen, I am thinking of you. All the time I am photocopying and making cups of coffee, I am playing each moment of last night's rapture over and over again in my mind. He believes that during working hours at least, he owns me; unaware that in my head, I am with you, in your bed, making love again and again and again.

And now the day is drawing to a close. As the night sky darkens outside, and the office murmur shifts to *plans -for-the-evening* and *one-last-thing-before-I-go*, I begin to prepare myself to return to you. The boss is leaving early, rushing home to see his kids in a school concert, and I am ready with my coat the minute he has gone. My feet race through the building, out into the chilly air, as I run to catch the bus to take me back to you. It is crowded, and I have to stand, holding onto the rail, texting one handed, *I am coming, I am coming, I am coming*. The journey is agonisingly slow; you are so close, but so far. It is too much, this waiting, this expectancy, it is too much. At last, I reach your stop. I alight, hurrying to the end of the street. Finally– your door. And there you are, at last framed in the hall light. You greet me with a kiss, and it's a good one; one that will last all night.

red shoes

The girl totters on the edge of the pavement. The heels on her red stilettos are high enough and thin enough that if she moves one inch forward she'll fall in front of the cars racing past her.

I feel like yelling, "Be careful, love!" but she won't hear me from down there. Instead I watch her trying to put her umbrella up. It looks like one of the crap ones from Poundland. No wonder it keeps blowing inside out. Despite the weather, she's wearing next to nothing – a thin white cardigan over a low cut blouse, a short black skirt, bare legs. She must be freezing dressed like that, yet she doesn't seem to notice. She just teeters on the brink of danger, looking like she's trying to decide something.

I used to dress like that, not caring about the wind and rain, so long as the look was right. I even had a pair of shoes to match: ruby red and glistening with fake diamonds. They were magic, my red shiny shoes, just one click of the heels and off we'd dance on another adventure: clubs, parties, concerts; we went everywhere together.

Why, once we even tripped off with a fella up to Blackpool to see the lights. Fantastic they were, and so was he. And he wasn't the only one, neither. My lucky shoes took me dancing, night after night, bloke after bloke. Lovely days they were. Till we danced into George. And after that, I didn't need no more excitement; I had enough right here at home. Life was like that for ever such a long time.

Of course, George and me, we don't get up to much these days. There's not much chance of shenanigans in such a tiny flat. And who wants to go out in this wind, when you need thermals just to go to the post office? I'm not that girl in the street no more. Those days are long gone.

The rain has eased off. She's put her brolly down. She turns her head slightly and gazes back this way. Perhaps she's looking at someone, her eyes rest on the flats next door. I'm probably making it up, but it seems to me she's saying goodbye. She turns back towards the road, as if she's come to a decision. Yes, she's taking a step onto the street. There she goes, dashing across the traffic on the dual carriageway. I watch her trip her way towards the tube. *You go, my girl* - I think - *click your heels and be off.*

The clock strikes five. The sun comes out from behind a cloud. Perhaps there'll be a rainbow in a minute. I don't have time to wait though. George needs his tea. He don't like it when I keep him waiting. I slip my red slippers back on and head to the kitchen. I think we'll have shepherd's pie tonight.

telling the family

The decision is made. In reality it was made a long time ago. Tonight was inevitable from the moment they met. Now it has happened - there is one thing left to do.

"When are we going to let everyone know?" asks Matt.

"You mean you haven't updated your Facebook status yet?" Jess grins.

Matt rarely lets a moment go by without telling the world. His enthusiasm for social media is one of the things she loves about him. He grins back at her, he loves her gentle teasing, it makes him feel part of their own special club. He pulls her closer to him on the sofa.

"Only, Mum said to come over at the weekend. I thought we could tell them then."

"You've been planning this." Jess looks at him appreciatively. "I like a Man with a Plan."

He laughs, and gives her a peck.

"No ... not really... It just seems like a good time to do it."

She kisses him back.

"It is a good time to do it."

She kisses him some more and soon they aren't thinking of anything except each other. Pretty soon they have rolled off the sofa against a pile of books waiting to be placed in the newly constructed shelf. *Lolita, Persuasion, Fifty Shades of Grey* scatter in the path of their rampant bodies.

At the time they barely notice the book spines pressing on their backs, though they will feel the bruises later. And it takes them a day to spot the Dan Brown is so stained it has to be thrown in the bin. Afterwards, they lie on the blue pile rug stroking each other's skin as if for the first time. It is only hunger and Matt's urgent need to pee that forces them off the floor.

By the time he returns, she is already dressed and is in the kitchen rifling through boxes.

"What are you looking for?" he asks as he pulls up his trousers.

"The frying pan."

"What are we having?"

"Omelette ... ah here it is," she finds it at the bottom of a blue crate.

"Yum. Champagne?"

"You really were prepared."

She begins to chop vegetables. He takes the bottle from the fridge, carefully twisting the cork until the moment of release. *Pop!* It shoots up to the ceiling covering them both in the sticky spray.

"Cheers." They clink glasses.

"Here's to the rest of our lives." Jess smiles.

The future lies ahead of her. Everything she's ever dreamt of right here in front of her eyes. It's going to be wonderful, she just knows it is.

"I can't wait to tell our parents," Matt smiles back, imagining the looks on their faces, the excitement they will feel. "I can't wait."

part two: what comes after

after the rapture

The sun is beginning to set behind them. Orange beams radiate from the top of the copse streaking a fiery path across the blue-grey ocean. Sylvie's back aches. Her knees ache. Her head aches. When she comes to think about it, everything aches, and has been aching all day. This is not the rapture he has promised her. They have been waiting for two hours for nothing to happen.

Jim is as silent as he was this morning; this time he has not been able to find the words to help her keep the faith. This time she is beginning to doubt. She looks at him in side profile: long nose, blue eyes, fair hair; a face she has loved for over a year. Tonight for the first time the treacherous thought creeps in, why, exactly? What is it about him that has made her abandon her life, her mother, her friends? His smile? The attention he pays her? His passionate conviction that God has been speaking to him, and him alone? Perhaps it is all three, but now his certainties have been vanquished, he suddenly seems as full of human frailties as everyone else. Sylvie aches. She has had enough. She wants to go home.

She is about to stand up, and tell him enough is enough, when he leaps to his feet.

"Do you hear it?" he says, his eyes shining.

"Hear what?"

All she can hear is the sound of the wind, the crash of the waves on the rocks below, the screeching of gulls in the air above them.

"Listen," he pulls her to her feet, "Close your eyes, and really listen."

"To what?"

"The angels singing."

Sylvie is torn between disbelief and faith. After all this time, she hates the idea of finding him wanting, fallible, human. But the truth is..."I can't hear anything."

"Sssh," he says stroking her hair, bringing her close to him. She can hear his heart beating. He is breathing deep calm breaths. "Listen," he says again, "Have faith. Listen."

Sylvie wants to have faith. She wants to believe. She closes her eyes, resting her head on his chest, letting it rise and fall with every breath he takes. And then, she hears it. Above the noise of the gulls, the crashing waves, the sighing wind, she hears it: the song of angels, pure, high, so beautiful she could cry with joy. She opens her eyes and sees tears in his.

"I hear them."

"They are calling to us. A final test."

"What?"

"We are the only ones left. Can you hear the thunder?" She nods, hearing the rumble in the distance behind them. "It's a sign. Everyone else is gone, the plagues and pestilence will be starting. Listen to the angels. We have to take this leap of faith."

He walks to the edge of the cliff, extending his arm to her.

"You mean jump?"

"The angels will carry us up to heaven. We just have to believe."

She looks at his radiant face, the rapture glowing in his

eyes. She doubts no more. She takes his hand and steps forward.

"I love you," she says.

"I love you too."

As she steps forward, he lets his hand drop. It is too late for her to stop, and she is falling through the air. The gulls screech, the wind sighs, the waves crash. The sky above her glowers with black clouds...

...and the angels have disappeared. Her last sight is of Jim standing, arms outstretched on top of the cliff, as if he is blessing her flight.

Jim watches her descent with something like regret; he has grown quite fond of Sylvie in recent months. But she was clearly suffering from the kind of doubt that would challenge his conclusion that the calculations were slightly out. And doubt cannot be tolerated. Already he is forming an account of the incident to ensure his followers will never doubt again.

She had more faith than me, he will say, *She took a leap of faith. Her earthly body was dashed on the rocks. But I saw her lifted up to heaven. For the rapture is not for all of us, we sinners are left behind. She had more faith than me. And she leapt.*

The story he tells the police will be somewhat different.

the jumper

The jumper is left draped over the futon with a casual
familiarity. He notices it minutes after she has left. The
jumper is turquoise, flecked with green. It looks
comfortable against the cushion, as if in this is the place it
should be when not adorning her long slender back. He
can't help feeling she has left it behind deliberately, as a
message: *Get in touch.*

He steps over to the sofa, picks it up, buries his face in
the wool. He wrinkles his nose in anticipation of her
smell, imagining lily-of-the-valley, soft, subtle - his
mother's favourite perfume. But the aroma exuding from
the left-behind garment is less fragrant. Cigarette smoke
and sweat. She hasn't washed it in weeks. Now he looks
close up he can see red soup stains by the V-shaped neck,
sugar crystals stuck to the mid-riff, and what appears to
be chocolate on the hem. He hasn't expected this. For a
moment he hesitates.

Then he remembers her smile as she left. He picks up
his mobile and texts: *You left your jumper behind. Shall I bring
it to you?* He sits back on the futon, hugging the jumper
close to him. It is a little piece of her. He knows he wasn't
imagining her interest in him. He cannot wait to return it,
to see her face, and be invited in for, well he hopes, for
more than just a cup of coffee.

She arrives at the bar and orders Pernod and black-currant. Tiny Tempeh is blaring out from the music system. It is still early. Soon this place will be full of Friday night screeching, but right now she has time to nip out the back for a quick fag. She has her pick of tables, so she chooses one furthest from the door. She takes the cigarette packet from her back pocket, pulls out a slender cigarette, caresses it. The lighter flares orange as she places the cigarette in her lips, lighting the tip. She drags in the sweet smell and breathes out a long sigh. The first fag of the evening is always the best – full of hope and desire, before a night's smoking causes her throat to rasp.

Though there are heaters in the courtyard, she has placed herself too far from them. That was stupid, it is November after all. She shivers, reaching in her bag for her jumper. It is not there. Where can she have left it? She retraces her steps in her mind. The post office? No, she wasn't wearing it then. The tube. She definitely didn't have it then. She knew she was wearing it at lunchtime because it was cold when she nipped out for a sandwich. She is still trying to work it out when a message blinks on her phone. *You left your jumper behind. Shall I bring it to you?* For a moment, she struggles to remember the number and then it comes to her. Jan's friend. The one who's DVDs she'd borrowed. She'd dropped them off earlier. She'd forgotten all about that.

She is about to text back, but the door into the patio opens. Her date for the evening.

"I thought I'd find you out here."

He smiles. She smiles back, shoving her phone in her bag. She'll phone wotsisname tomorrow. There's no rush.

It will take him three weeks of persistent texting to arrange a meeting that will last exactly five minutes. His love will last a few seconds more.

now what is love?

If this isn't love, it is something very like: Friday Night at the Fridge. The sweaty dance floor pulsates with bodies pressing us together in the darkness. This physical closeness is new and exciting. We are slow dancing to Squeeze: my arms around your neck, my fingers ruffling your afro; your arms around my waist, your hands fondling my bum. Though it goes against everything I've ever been taught, I am letting you touch me wherever you want. Nothing will stop me from going back with you tonight. When we leave I will call Mum and Dad from the phone box by Brixton Station. They will believe me when I say I'm staying at Emma's. I am their good little girl, I never lie. Instead I will follow you to your basement flat, lie down upon your double bed, let your hands move under the frills of my ra-ra skirt and ...I cannot quite imagine what happens next, it is too far outside my experience. It doesn't matter. After tonight, everything changes. After tonight, I will know what it is to truly love.

This is love isn't it? Everyone is gawping at me – a perfect bride in my virginal-white, puffed-sleeve, fake Diana dress – as I glide down the aisle on my Dad's arm. Allegedly, he is supporting me, but in reality, I am supporting him. I know he wants to see me settled before

– well we don't like to say it or think it, but we all know there's not much time left. I don't want to let him or Mum down, and yet my smile is hesitant when I reach you. I can't quite be sure your returning smile is entirely for my benefit. When the best man's wife reads the words chosen by my parents (living proof that love is not jealous, boastful or unkind), I want to believe that you are staring at the lectern and not her breasts. My voice trembles as we make our vows; my hands shake with the exchange of rings; we are man and wife and the church erupts with joy. The sheer exuberance sweeps my doubts away; I have made this bed, I *will* delight in it.

Love is not this jealous, *should* not be this jealous. You say you work so hard during the week you need to go out clubbing to relax. You never ask if *I* want to relax. Every time you stay out till four in the morning, I lie awake, wondering which girl you have gone home with this week. I picture you lying down in her bed, your hands up her skirt, till I cannot bear to imagine anymore.

Last Friday, when I was bathing the baby, I noticed you'd left your ring by the soap. When I asked you, you said you forgot it in the rush; tonight it's there again, even though you took your time. You always have a plausible explanation for the strange phone calls: the ones where the other caller hangs up when I answer, or you change the subject when I walk in the room. I'd love to believe you, but I can't. Instead, I am left here, holding the baby, trying to remember that love bears all things, believes all things, hopes all things. Asking myself: can I?

Whatever love is, it's not this... If your Friday nights at the Fridge were selfish fifteen years ago, today they just seem sad. I have long given up on self-deceit. I know you for what you are now Leroy: a forty year old balding sexual predator, stalking girls not much older than your daughters. I have thought so often of leaving, written you a thousand walkout letters in my mind, but I can't quite bring myself to do it. It would upset Mum for a start, who still clings to the delusion that love endures. It would hurt the girls, who despite everything still believe in the fading glamour that lingers around you. It might even hurt me. For sometimes after a late shift in the pub, I find you sleeping on the sofa, a book of photography on your stomach, a glass of whisky by your side. On those nights you almost look like someone I could love. And then I remind myself, that I was the one who made this bed. Isn't up to me to have the patience – to hope that love, after all, might still abide?

This is not love. I doubt it ever was. But old habits die hard. It is Friday night and you are down the Fridge as usual: a fifty something clubber with a knee replacement, a paunch, and seedy charm. It's no longer sad, it's sordid. I cannot think that you have anything to offer anyone but sexual disease and misery. I feel sorry for your victims, but they are no longer my concern. My difficulty is this. Each Friday, I sit in the house we've lived in for thirty years, listening to the Squeeze CD you bought me in a rare moment of sentimentality, pondering my walkout note. There is nothing to keep me here. Mum is dead; the girls left long ago. There is no reason for me to stay and yet old habits die hard for me too. It's not that I love you, or ever will again. It's just that somehow, after all this time, I have lost the ability to live my life differently. This is not love. I doubt it ever was. But, somehow, despite myself, it endures.

night watch

The moon is bright tonight. Its pale beams pick out the contours of your face: the soft curve of your chin, the gentle bump of your lips, the hillock of your nose. I am a fitful sleeper, I like to watch you on nights like this, when you are in a deep sleep, still wrapped in the warmth of our recent lovemaking. Watching as you dream the foolish dreams of a contented lover: full of memories of the evening that has just past and anticipation of the nights that are yet to come. You turn over, and sigh, a deep, satisfied sigh. I am everything you have ever wanted. I will fulfil your every need.

You don't know it yet, but I am trouble, with a capital "T". Your friends sense it, as friends always do – the iceberg that lurks beneath my still, calm waters. But by the time they get close enough to expose the danger you are in, it will be too late to send up flares. By then I will have run you aground, your lower decks crumpled, as you begin to sink into my icy depths. They will be desperate in their bids to save you, but their pathetic attempts will come to nothing. Life jackets, rubber rings and tiny boats will flounder in the black waters and be consumed by the waves. For you will give them up, each and every one of them. You will reject their years of love and loyalty in favour of your mistaken belief in me – your inability to see that I am trouble with a capital "T".

I like watching your face at night time. I like to see you

still and peaceful, completely oblivious that I have the power to choose both the time and manner of your ending. Sometimes, on a particularly insomniac night, I wonder if I should pity you. But even as your steady breaths form tiny clouds in the cold air of your unheated flat, I know that pity is impossible. All I have ever had to offer anyone is ice and fog – why should you be any different? The moon sinks across the horizon, drowning in the morning clouds that turn black, purple and pale blue. From the east, the first orange rays of sun drift across your face, warming you awake. You smile and murmur as I lean over to kiss you. Your waking grin is as generous as it is foolish.

"Happy New Year," you say.

"Happy New Year. It's going to be a good one."

You beam back, content in the happiness that is to come this year, enjoying the sight of me getting dressed. I smile back with all the warmth that you deserve.

I am trouble, with a capital "T". You just don't know it yet.

brush strokes

It's the fiddly bits that get you when painting. The parts between wall and ceiling where you can't rely on your rollers anymore. Where you have to stretch arms, strain your neck, stand on tiptoe to ensure your paint brush doesn't fleck the ceiling or corner wall as you attempt a neat finish. A perfect line between purple, white and green. It helps to have a wet rag handy, ready to wipe away splodges and mis-strokes. You've been doing this for years now, you know the score. Though nowadays when you come down you'll have lower back ache, sore calves and aching shoulders. You are not as young as you were.

Later in the bath, as you sip a glass of wine, you remember watching Harry paint that first house in Blenheim Yard. You were hugely pregnant, happy to watch him as he turned the nursery blue for the boy you both imagined you were having. As he came down from the step-ladder he tripped, knocking the paint which splattered blue stains across the new white carpet. He fell in it, rolling around till his face was covered with woad.

You laughed, and laughed. You could not stop till your waters broke and the next blue was the flashing light of the ambulance that rushed you to hospital where Jenny was born three hours later. The unexpected girl, instead of the boy you never did have. Perhaps that was part of the problem. At the time it didn't seem to matter, when you arrived home, Harry had cleaned the carpet and the walls were perfectly pink.

It was when you moved house to accommodate the expanding family (Helena, two years after Jenny, then Millie, and finally Emma) that you needed to take up the brush yourself. Harry was too busy at work to help around the house anymore. You didn't begrudge his trips abroad, the long evenings by yourself. It paid for ballet lessons, drama clubs, school trips. The least you could do, when you were alone and the children were sleeping, was give the girls' bedrooms the makeovers they deserved. Pink, purple, red. The colours changed with the ages, and the fads they went through. Though you drew the line at black when Millie and Emma went all emo just before they left school.

It's funny, you think, as you get back to the job the next morning, in all these years, the one room you never got round to was your own. It takes a husband leaving to do that. Now as you finish the final corner, you step down from your ladder and look round with pride. Purple, green and white: suffragette colours.

Life begins.

liberation

The bus rattled along the bumpy road, through miles of brown rock and pink dust. It was not the image of desert I'd had in mind when Lee suggested the trip. I knew it was irrational to feel disappointed when we reached the oasis on the outskirts of the town. But images of palm trees, shimmering water, camels and sand dunes were hard to shake off. Mud, a trickle of water, and scraggy trees were poor substitutes.

We struggled off the bus, sitting at the side of the road to check our Lonely Planet. A couple of hawkers drifted up, hopefully. We were old hands by now and brushed them away. They took their collections of purses and beaded necklaces down to the gate of big hotel, lying in wait for the rich tourists. We were hot, thirsty, and our clothes were full of dust. Not for the first time, I wished we had money. How pleasant it would be to sink into clean sheets, an air conditioned room, and a swim in the cool pool. Our destination, as always, was the heart of the medina - a narrow terraced hotel, with a small bed, squat toilet, a 50:50 chance of a shower.

I picked Lee up in a bank in Casablanca. We got chatting in the queue and it seemed natural to go for lunch afterwards. When we discovered we were both heading to Marrakech, it was the easiest thing in the world to join forces. A relief, too. I was getting tired of the incessant stream of men following me around. A man at my side was a talisman to ward off their advances. As we journeyed south on the train, watching the green fields leach into stony red mountains, it was pleasant to lean my head against his, sharing life stories. The night was clear; the moon, full. The landscape would have been dreary by day, but that evening the rocks and boulders sparkled like jewels as the shafts of light bounced between them. It seemed to me, at that moment, that Lee was the greatest treasure of them all.

Three weeks later, and Marrakech had lost its charm. There are only so many trips to the souk, so many snake charmers, so many bowls of couscous. Even sunset, at the top of the Cafe de France watching the lights of the city come on, one by one as the muezzins called, was passé. I didn't need much urging to get out of town, and head south to the Sahara, a journey I might not have made alone. But now we were here, I couldn't help resenting the way Lee automatically took charge. I sighed, reminding myself it would still be worth it for the sight of sunrise over the dunes.

The hotel was like all the rest, on a narrow side street off the main square. A plain reception desk with blue and white tiles behind. Rooms off a central courtyard that still retained the heat of the day, even after nightfall. A morose man on the desk, who spoke only to Lee, as I tried, and failed, to not feel excluded. We dragged our rucksacks up to the bedroom and threw ourselves on the bed. It was good to stop moving for a while.

We struck lucky on the shower front. That at least was a blessing. Once we'd washed, we had the energy to forage for food. As we crossed the courtyard, a woman emerged from a door at the back of the hotel. She was wearing a long purple dress, her head covered in a lilac hijab. She was carrying a bowl of couscous and tajine, which she took to the man on the desk. She spoke to him briefly and then scurried back, not looking at us as she passed.

"What a life." I said, as we walked down the street, trying not to wrinkle our noses at the smell of rotting rubbish.

"What do you mean?"

"Waiting on a man too lazy to get his own food. Covering yourself up to avoid his censure. In the twenty first century too. So submissive."

"Seems alright to me." Lee joked. I nudged him in the ribs, and we continued on our way.

At bedtime we lay naked, on top of the bedclothes. It was too hot to make love. Outside the army trucks rumbled through the town. Occasionally we heard people shouting somewhere in the street. I tossed and turned, and wished myself a million miles away. My sense of adventure was deserting me. All I wanted was cool air and sleep. I got little of either. By the time the muezzin called at five, I was tired and grouchy, a mood that didn't improve as the day progressed. We left after breakfast seeking a Grands Taxi, something Lee had assured me would be easy. But he hadn't factored for a two day conference at the desert hotel; when we arrived at the sun-blistered square there were no taxis to be found. We waited and waited as the heat gradually built to sauna levels, the only relief found in a shaded corner, where we drank ice cold coke, played cards, and bickered about how long we should stay. When a battered six-seater Mercedes finally appeared in the late afternoon, Lee refused to contemplate paying the full price, and my dream of the desert was over. There was nothing for it but to head back to the hotel where our argument lasted most of the night. The next day, we took the bus back to Marrakech, bouncing along the dusty roads in silence; I could hardly bear to look at him.

"Same place as before?" Lee asked, when we reached our destination. It galled me to still be relying on him, but I didn't have the energy for independence tonight. "Separate beds." He nodded. We picked up our bags and staggered through the crowded streets to the tiny hotel.

Leaving him could wait till morning.

silver wedding

The table cloth comes out every year. Of course it does. The famous Arkwright lace. The fabric that founded a dynasty. Each anniversary, it must be carried from the top drawer of the tallboy in the second guest bedroom, where it has lain for twelve months in laundered anticipation, and unfolded on the ebony table in the dining room in our honour. What better way to celebrate our love?

It was with us from the start. Decorating the table throughout the awkward wedding reception. My parents, overwhelmed by the grandeur, hardly daring to say a word. Your parents taking centre stage, allowing us our brief moments of glory - toasts, your speech, cake cutting - in between their beguiling tales of family history. The cloth emerged the following year at the anniversary meal your mother insisted on throwing, even though I'd have preferred a quiet night in, just the two of us. The following year, we *couldn't possibly* disappoint her because your father was so ill and she needed something else to think about. And the next, when the baby meant we were too exhausted to organise anything ourselves and it would have been churlish to refuse. And the next, and the next...till the ritual was carved in tablets of stone so that, even after your mother's death, it is preserved through the machinations of the elder sisters you dare not disappoint.

Now here we are again. Twenty five years after the original event. Twenty five years? My, my, how time has flown. And haven't we been having *so* much fun? Here we are again, climbing the steps of the house, ringing that ridiculous clanging bell. Here's Daphne, taking my coat with her usual smile of disdain for my fashion sense. Here's Georgia, handing out the cocktails, as we make polite conversation. Here's her dull husband Steven, and Daphne's duller husband Edwin, and a coterie of Arkwrights who are wheeled out for the occasion. Our grown up children trailing behind us. It is kind of them to come, but I wouldn't blame them if one year they exercised their right of refusal.

Dinner is served, as always, in the red dining room. The long table ordained with the white, crisp cotton and floral loops of lace that the family admires so. As ever, it is when we sit down to eat, that the stories begin...How the cloth was created in honour of the wedding of Joshua Arkwright's first born son and has been used for every Arkwright nuptial since. How a lazy servant nearly ruined it by not taking it to the laundress immediately after spillage of white wine - an error remedied by the watchful housekeeper who sacked the servant on the spot and took it herself. How Great Uncle Charlie (dreary in life - the stuff of legend in death) rescued it from burning when the west wing of the house caught fire. My only role in proceedings is to smile and nod, though in my head I fantasise about setting fire to it myself. Or taking a knife and ripping those lace whorls to shreds. Better still, I think that if I were to just knock the waiter's right arm a fraction, the red wine would flow across the table discolouring every fibre, like a deep purple wound. I'm not sure if it's lack of courage, or unwillingness to destroy a beautiful artefact, but as always, something stays my hand.

The evening meanders on. Boring chit chat, interlaced with a fine cut of beef, meringues that melt in the mouth, and cheese that has almost liquefied by the time it reaches me. At last, the final morsel is consumed, the last story told, and it is time for the inevitable speeches. Here's Daphne, toasting her baby brother, and Georgia, raising a glass to me, the ever youthful wife. Here are you, rising in response thanking your siblings and the Arkwright family for their annual generosity. And here am I playing my part in our happy anniversary, gazing at you with the requisite amount of adoration as you conclude, "Twenty-five glorious years, here's to twenty five more." I smile down at the applauding table, noting the offending cloth littered with the debris of the evening, and it occurs to me that I've had my fill of family myths and sagas. Our lives have been weighed with the burden of history for far too long. Next year, I *must* put my foot down. Twenty five years *has* to be enough. Next year, we're going to do our own thing. I *really* mean it this time. *Next year*, I promise myself, it's Benidorm or bust.

happy birthday, darling

I know, the minute I see it, what the present is. You always play this silly game of pretending it is something else, wrapping the statue in a big box, or a cylinder, or once in a Quality Streets tin, in a vain attempt to hide the tell-tale shape. But I know what it is, of course I do. It's a Dresden shepherdess, another fucking shepherdess. I bet I know which one it is too. The silly curtseying girl with the posy. The one that was at the centre of my grand-mother's collection. Out of all the loathsome ornaments on her mantelpiece, that was the worst of the lot - the smile, the posy, the curtsey, all implying some deference to a man, or a lord, or lady, an attitude I have no time for.

It was sweet - at first - this attempt to please me. I was touched that day we met in George and Alice's living room to discover you had been there when I watched the statues tumble down the steps. Touched by your interest, and to know how you'd empathised with my upset. When, on our first anniversary, you bought me my first statue, I didn't have the heart to tell you, that though you'd heard my story, you hadn't listened properly. You were so sure the gift would make me happy; I couldn't bear to disappoint you. Couldn't bear to let you know you had missed the point entirely. I should have been tougher then, told you that you hadn't listened. But this was in the early days of our love, before I realised you never listen, and that our life together would be built on foundations of misunderstanding, bricks of incomprehension, roofed by your lack of self-awareness.

You're a quiet man - I understand that; it's what once drew me to you. After Tim, and Geoffrey, Richard and Sam, I was sick of men who put themselves at the centre. You seemed to me to be of a different sort altogether. I mistook your silence, and concern for my past distress as signs of an empathetic temperament. A mistake, as foolish as the smile of the girl that emerges as I unwrap the damned statue. Empathy, I have discovered the hard way, is not in your nature. You didn't cry, as I did, when we lost our first baby. And, by the time I lost the third, you couldn't even look me in the eye. You wouldn't try IVF. After you'd researched it, and calculated the probabilities, you were sure it would be a waste of time; and once you've made up your mind on something, there's no shifting you. I gave up on the argument long ago, threw my energies into my PR consultancy, watched it grow and develop in ways I couldn't have imagined at the start. And all the time conscious of this gaping hole in my life, a hole invisible to you, but one that no amount of theatre tickets or foreign holidays can fill.

Meanwhile, on every birthday, and anniversary, and Christmas, you present me with yet another statue, yet another sodding shepherdess. Once you've made up your mind there's no shifting you; and you decided long ago, that you would help me recreate the collection I have lost. You silly, silly man. You didn't listen. You never listen. I wasn't crying for the loss of those damn ornaments that day; I always hated the bloody things. I wept because my grandma had left them to me in her will, and as I watched them tumble down the steps, it was like watching her die all over again. I wept because that was my last physical connection to her, and once broken, I could no longer pretend to myself her death was not absolute. I wept with the knowledge she was gone, and gone for good. But after you left the scene, and Tim helped me clear up, as we wrapped the broken pieces, and places them in the bin, the sadness passed. I realised they were just statues, after all, and ones I'd never liked. I moved on with my life and never thought of them again, until you began this torment of unwanted gifts.

I smile politely (do you not sense how strained my smile is?) and thank you for your present, taking it to the fourth bed room, where it will sit with the rest. (Have you not noticed that that is the room that I never enter?) Today, for the sake of the peace, I will pretend to enjoy my birthday spoils. Tomorrow, I intend to sell the lot.

waiting for the thaw

"The path needs doing again."

"Uh,huh." He looked out of the window at the snow flakes falling from the darkening grey sky, obliterating the track that sloped down to the road, where even the four by fours were struggling to keep moving. It was only an hour since he'd last cleared it, but already another two inches had fallen. The snow drifts on the lawn had risen to seven or eight inches and were so densely packed that they were almost reaching the bottom window panes.

"I said the path needs doing again."

This time her voice was edged with insistence.

He did not look up from force of habit, but simply turned over the page of the paper he was reading.

"It's Someone Else's Turn."

She rose from her seat and walked, back erect, with deliberately paced steps to the door.

"I won't repeat myself. I have supper to cook."

She departed down the stone-flagged corridor for the kitchen.

He sighed, put down his paper and followed her into the dark hallway where the heat of the radiators barely penetrated. His Barbour jacket was still damp from his last outing; his boots were icy when he put them on. He picked up the spade he'd left by the front door, and went outside.

The job took longer than expected. His back and

knees were not what they were; stabbing him with pain each time he bent over. The snow fell almost as fast as he could clear it. Large wet flakes splattered his eyes, blinding him, so he had to stop and wipe them every couple of minutes. It was frustrating work, but the dread of being snowed in was enough to keep him at it. He dug and scraped until the path was clear. Though by the time he'd stood at the door for a couple of minutes to shake the snow from his boots, the path was white again.

She heard the metal scraping the pathway as she busied herself around the kitchen. At least he was getting *that* job done. The weekly shop had not been done that morning, and they'd not be able to get out tomorrow. She probably had enough for a couple of decent meals. After that – well it would have to be soup and dry crackers. Tonight, at least, there were two lamb cutlets to use up, and enough potatoes and peas to make it feel like a proper supper. They'd run out gravy, but that couldn't be helped.

She heard the clang of the spade against the wall as he closed the front door.

"Supper will be five minutes," she called.

"Uh, huh."

"I said, 'Supper will be five minutes'."

Her yell had more insistence in it.

"I heard you the first time. I'm just changing my trousers."

Thud, thud, thud. He climbed the stairs as she took the cutlets out of the oven and put them on the plates. She sieved the steaming potatoes, and dabbed them with butter, watching it melt into yellow liquid running down through the pan. Typically, he was still not down when she put the peas on the plates. She put the food back in the oven till she heard his thudding descent.

As he entered the room, she placed the plates back on the table, and they both sat down.

"There's no gravy," he said

"Someone didn't go to the shops."

He said nothing more; they ate in their usual silence. The only sounds were his masticating jaws, the clink of cutlery, and, outside, the snow-muffled engines of the last cars to make into the village tonight.

She knew the food was delicious, but though he ate his quickly enough, as usual he could never be bothered to compliment her. When he'd finished his final mouthful, he pushed away the plate, rose from the table and disappeared to watch the news. She cleared the table, as was her custom, and began to wash up.

Clink, splash, wipe, clink, splash, wipe. There was something soothing about washing up at the end of the day. Outside the snow kept on falling. The sky was black.

"They say this is going to last till Thursday at least," he called from the living room.

"Uh, huh," she said, looking at the ice that was beginning to form on the steaming window.

It would be a long time till the thaw.

alive-alive-o

Tell yourself. You're *pleased* Cassie got the promotion. Really. Now you can live in the white house on the hill. The one you both dreamed of when you were kids on the beach. Large. Clean. Warm. Not like the fucking boxes the army gave you. The walls so thin, you heard every word of the neighbour's domestics. As they heard yours.

Tell yourself. You're fucking *lucky* mate. She took you back, didn't she? Again. After everything *you've* done. You didn't deserve a second chance, and she's given you a fifth. Anyone else would have walked away long ago. Not Cassie. She's a diamond. One in a million. You're lucky, mate, you really are.

Tell yourself. You don't care about the way the girls look at you. That they don't speak to you. Or mind you, unless their mother says. Whose fucking fault is that? Besides, teenage girls *never* speak to their fathers. Somewhere, under the piles of mascara and eye shadow, they still love you. They'll come round. Eventually.

Tell yourself. It doesn't matter that the job stinks. That *you* stink. Of cockles and mussels alive-a-fucking-o. It's a start isn't it? At least you have money of your own again. Don't have to rely on Cassie's wage. With your track record, it's a miracle anyone would ever employ you. It'll do for now. Till something better comes along.

Tell yourself. As you pass the tourists packing out the pubs and avoid the offie on the way home from work. As you sit in the evening watching crap on TV. As you lie awake, in the middle of the night, wondering what the fuck happened to your life. Tell yourself. Like they told you in the clinic: I don't need a drink.

Perhaps, one day, it will be true.

hesitation

I should leave now. I really should. There's nothing here to keep me. The party ended a long time ago. All that remains are the scattered crumbs of former pleasures: fading wine stains; crumpled beer cans; the faint scent of stale cigarettes.

I should leave. I Should. Really. Leave. Now.

But still I hesitate. Pacing up and down our narrow hallway, rolling my black suitcase back and forth over the red carpet. Occasionally a wheel snags on the frayed edges, causing me to pause in my pointless journey. As I stop to untangle it, I wonder why I am still here. It can't be out of any desire to stay. To remain in the hangover of a now that has long past the point of no return to what once was.

Perhaps I am tempted by the tantalising illusion that what might be. That somehow we could still create a future where the bitterness of now is long forgotten, replaced by a magic that could be even better than what once was.

Or is it fear holding me back? The sense that what will be is bound to be a hell far worse than what is. The terror that if I leave, I will find myself yearning for the life I endure now, as much as I now long for the life that what once was.

From the kitchen, the oven clock beeps - seven o'clock - reminding me that the time to choose is passing. Before your feet tramp up the path, before your key turns in the lock I must be unpacked or be gone.

Back or Forth? Once or Future? Now or Never? It is time to make up my mind.

I really should be going. Really. I should.

a man's job

It's a man's job to provide for his family. That's what my father always taught me. That's what my mother always said. That was the reason Father worked all those long hours in the office, so that when I was tiny I sometimes didn't see him for five or six days. It was the reason Mother was always the one to meet us boys at the school gate. The reason she was the one who cooked the meals, darned the socks, soothed sick brows. *That* was Mother's job. It was what was expected of her. Father's role was to pay the bills for our expensive private schools, fund music lessons, acting classes and scout trips. His time with us limited to Sunday afternoon rugby matches, shouting from the sidelines, making sure we didn't let the side down. Is it any surprise that I grew up thinking that was what fathers did? What they were. Strong. Reliable. An absence so powerful the very mention of their names struck terror in naughty childish hearts. I had no doubts whatsoever that this is what I would become.

It certainly seemed that way, didn't it Steffi, my love? Though, being a modern father, I couldn't escape attendance at the grimacing births, or changing the obligatory nappies, the natural order quickly asserted itself once the paternity leave was done. I spent long days at the office, leaving you at home, with the job you claimed fulfilled you. A job that you have always claimed you loved. You may wail plaintively now, but for all that you chose me for who I am: an alpha male, with a six figure salary, and a media profile. You needed me to fund the lifestyle of *your* choosing: the country house, the chance to redecorate every year, the three foreign holidays you could brag about to your friends. Most of all, you wanted me at work, so you could establish your power base: the stranglehold you hold over home and hearth that has rendered me isolated, a stranger to my own family.

There have been times in the last ten years, I have wanted to protest. Times when the late night deals have palled, and I'd rather be at home with you and the kids, cuddling in front of the television. Weekends when I've found myself redundant – as I've watched you race from activity to activity assuring me I'd only be in the way. Moments when I've felt excluded from a relationship with my own children, because you have somehow created a situation where you are everything to them, and I am not. But, I've said nothing, accepting it as the way of things, or – vaguely aware now from conversations with other men that not every relationship is like this – the way of things in our house. I have done my duty by you, delivered home the bacon, created the life you wanted. I have always been the man you have wanted me to be.

And now, after all I have done for you, after all these years, you tell me you are leaving. It is now that you tell me that when I thought I was giving you exactly what you wanted I was doing just the opposite. Now that I learn that I have held you back, confined you to the kitchen sink, prevented you from realising your dreams. Your divorce citation makes pretty reading. *A tyrant, a bully, who forced me to stay at home, not letting me work.* And your behaviour has been a revelation. First you lock me out of the house bought with *my* money. Then you casually tell me you are moving to the other side of the country to be with the new man who has conveniently just showed up in your life. Now you are trying to deny me access to my own children, claiming they have no interest in seeing me, their own father.

I have a feeling that you think I'll take this lying down. You have clearly held me in such contempt for so long you believe that you have neutered me. You think I no longer pose a threat to you.

You underestimate me. You have forgotten, you see, how I was taught it was a man's job to be strong, reliable, and above all powerful. You have forgotten, that in the years you have sidelined me, I have not been unobservant. I have taken notes. The affairs you imagine you kept hidden from me. The drinking you think is a secret between you and the housekeeper. The moments when the perfect image has slipped, and you have revealed the raging, hysterical woman underneath. And you have forgotten, haven't you, that in those days you had a pet name for me.

You are so sure you have neutered me, you do not realise I am still your lion.

Watch me roar.

bad timing

"I don't think I love you anymore."

These are not words a girl wants to hear. Particularly, when the person uttering them is still inside you and you are experiencing the after-shocks of a deep and satisfying orgasm. Trust him to ruin a beautiful moment.

"Then you'd better go."

He doesn't move.

"*Now.*"

I push him off me. He rolls over to the damp side of the mattress.

"I'm sorry."

I am sure he is working up to saying he didn't mean to say it just then, it just came out. But I've heard that excuse in previous arguments. I really don't need it now.

"Save it."

"I wish——."

"Just *go.*"

He makes no further attempt at civilised conversation. Taking me at my word, he climbs out of bed, and grabs his clothes. I bury my head under the pillow so I don't have to look at him. But I can hear the crackle of static as he pulls a T Shirt over the torso that I was just stroking, the sliding of trousers up the legs that were so recently wrapped round my body.

" 'Bye then."

His words penetrate the muffle of the pillow case. If

he's looking for a moment of understanding or forgiveness I'm not inclined to give it. I wait till he has left the room before I allow myself to bring my head up to breathe. A sickly smell of sex pervades the room. It makes me gag. The door to the flat bangs. My cue to jump out of bed, run to the toilet and throw up.

I feel better for a second. And then I begin to cry. My body shakes with sobs that seem to surface from deep in my gut. What am I going to do now?

I don't know how long I sit there crying on the cold bathroom floor, my sticky legs rubbing against each other, aggravating my eczema. I do know that when the tears finally subside, and I pull myself up, my face is puffed and blotchy.

The stupid thing is, that sitting here alone like this, I know he is right. He doesn't love me. He never did. And I didn't love him either. We were held together by sex and the need for company on a Saturday night. Would it have made a difference if I'd said it first?

I have a shower, get dressed and make myself some toast. It doesn't change anything, so I phone in sick. I download *Casablanca* from Netflix, wrap myself in a blanket, and settle down to watch.

The bedroom will smell of sex for days. The bed-sheets will stay stained. Let them. I'm not going to clean up just yet.

the moves you make

"It's Sunday night, and you're listening to Allen Greene's *Sunday Smoochers*. First up, it's Suzy. Who's your dedication for Suzy?"

"Annie."

"Tell us about Annie."

"She's gorgeous. She has long brown hair, deep green eyes, I love her to bits."

"And where did you meet her?"

"At Leeds University, at the Freshers Ball. I saw her across the dance floor and couldn't stop watching her..."

"So, it was love at first sight?"

"Exactly. I told her she belonged to me, and that was it."

"Aaah. That's the kind of smooching story we like on this show... So what do you want to me to play, Suzy?"

"For my wonderful Annie, for five glorious years – The Police and *Every Breath You Take*. Cos, Annie, every single day, I'll be watching you."

"Great choice, thanks Suzy, Police coming right up..."

Annie takes in a deep breath and fights back an urge to run to the door. It's locked as always, and the curtains are drawn. She can't get in. She's made sure that woman can *never* get in. But ... how did she know? How did Suzy know what radio station Annie listened to? That she'd be listening tonight? Was she hacking into Annie's air waves? Was that even possible? She turns off the radio and hurtles it across the room. Every move she makes... That's another simple pleasure Suzy's ruined.

She runs into her bedroom, and dives under the cover, as if the embrace of the duvet can fight off the cold that is seeping through her bones. She knows from bitter experience that she'll hardly sleep tonight. If she does, her dreams will be full of endless flight and the question racing through her brain. How did Suzy know? How did she know? Then it dawns on her... Oh shit, Annie told her. She *bloody* told her. Back at the beginning, when Suzy was just a random friend on Facebook. She'd been sitting at home listening to the radio on her laptop on. She'd posted something about liking *Careless Whisper* and a couple of people had said they were listening too. That's when she'd said, in one little comment for the whole world to see: *Favourite show. Every Sunday. Always listening.* One little comment that Suzy has stored away for four years. Until now. Just when Annie was beginning to feel she'd escaped her, was beginning to feel safe. It is clear now that she isn't and she never will be. She might change jobs, cities, radio stations, but if Suzy's prepared to wait this long to use one tiny nugget of information, she's not going to stop, ever.

It doesn't matter what she does, where she goes. Every move she makes. Every breath she takes. Suzy will be watching. Always.

telling the family

The decision is made. In fact, it was made a long time ago. Tonight is just confirmation of the inevitable. Now it has happened, there is one thing left to do.

"When are we going to let everyone know?" asks Shirley.

"You mean you haven't updated your Facebook status yet?"

To an outsider Steve's voice always appears jovial. The snide intention behind such comments is pitched at a level audible to Shirley alone. It is comments like that – years of comments like that – she resists the inward fume and forces her mouth into a smile.

"Only the kids are coming this weekend. I thought we could tell them then."

"You've been planning this."

It is Steve's turn to fume – manipulative as ever – she has forced this to

happen exactly when it suits her.

"No ... not really... Look we've both known for a long time, haven't we...?" but she's lost him already.

He is staring at the bookcase as if he is already calculating how to divide the spoils of thirty years. No doubt he will try to claim the heavy stuff – what he calls "real literature" : Nabokov, Proust, Calvi – leaving her with the thriller collection: Francis, Grisham, Forsyth and the Dickens novels which he regards as overrated soap opera.

Perhaps she should let him. It seems to her this is one of

the more impossible acts of separation: dividing books that they've both enjoyed and given each other over the years. Then she thinks of how she was the one who introduced him to Will Self, to Borges, to Marquez, and sets her jaw in anticipation of the fight.

Steve continues his perusal of the shelves. He has some plastic boxes in his den. He has estimated their dimensions and now he is trying to work out how many books he will need per box. He cannot imagine how they will split the collection apart.

He gave her half of them. Should he claim them back? Doubtless, she will fight tooth and nail for the thrillers which she always enjoys on holiday, leaving him with the turgid books she thinks he likes – the foreign writers with their overblown prose and complicated storytelling. Shirley interrupts his train of thought.

"So, Saturday then? When the kids come?"

He grunts the grunt of resigned acceptance. The sooner he lets her have her own way, the sooner he can go his. He rises from the chair, departing upstairs for his den, where he will drink beer and watch *Game of Thrones* till the small hours.

Shirley watches his retreating back with relief. Time was when she couldn't have borne him leaving her even for a minute. When the rapture of being together meant everything. But times change, and so have they. For every tale of everlasting love, you'll find another full of heartbreak and misery. And she's had enough of that. Now he's gone, she can revel in the delight of an evening to herself. She wanders into the kitchen, pours a glass of wine, and raises it silently: *Here's to the rest of my life.* After the weekend, she'll be on her own for good.

She can't wait.

Acknowledgements

Many of these stories first appeared on my blog as part of the weekly "Friday Flash" writing community. I'd like to thank all my fellow "flashers" for their encouragement, in particular, Marc Nash, John Wiswell, Icy Sedgwick, Maria Protopapadaki-Smith, Cathy Oliffe-Webster and Lou Freshwater whose opinions I value and whose fiction I highly recommend. Also to my lovely friend Anne Booth who has so often given positive feedback and everyone else who has read and commented.

When I was contemplating self-publishing, my twin sister, Julia William did a brilliant first edit and critique which gave me the confidence that these were stories worth telling. Thanks so much.

I would also like to thank the following:

Calum Kerr at Gumbo Press for taking me on in the first place, for being a fine editor, designer and typesetter.

My parents Ann and Joseph Moffatt aren't around to see this collection published, but I would never have been brave enough to be a writer without their constant encouragement.

My siblings John, Joanna, Paula, Lucy, Julia, Hugh and Tom who have cheered me on for years. I'm glad I finally have something to show for it.

My children, Beth, Claire and Jonathan, who offer excellent critique of my writing and constant enthusiasm about my work and prospects.

And finally, my wonderful husband Chris, who first pointed out "Friday Flash" to me and who always provides constant back up and support. Couldn't do it without you.

Other books from **Gumbo Press**:

www.gumbopress.co.uk

The Book of Small Changes
by Tim Stevenson

This collection takes its inspiration from the Chinese I Ching: where the sea mourns for those it has lost, encyclopaedia salesmen weave their accidental magic, and the only true gift for a king is the silence of snow.

Enough by Valerie O'Riordan

Fake mermaids and conjoined twins, Johannes Gutenberg, airplane sex, anti-terrorism agricultural advice, Bluebeard and more.
Ten flash-fictions.

Threshold by David Hartley

Threshold explores the surreal and the strange through thirteen flash-fictions which take us from a neighbour's garden, out into space, and even as far as Preston. But which Preston?

Undead at Heart by Calum Kerr

War of the Worlds meets *The Walking Dead* in this novel from Calum Kerr, author of *31* and *Braking Distance*

The World in a Flash: How to Write Flash Fiction by Calum Kerr

A guide for beginners and experienced writers alike to give you insight into the world of flash-fiction. Chapters focus on a range of aspects, with exercises for you to try.

The 2014 Flash365 Collections
by Calum Kerr

Apocalypse
It's the end of the world as we know it. Fire is raining from the sky, monsters are rising from the deep., and the human race is caught in the middle.

The Audacious Adventuress
Our intrepid heroine, Lucy Burkhampton, is orphaned and swindled by her evil nemesis, Lord Diehardt. She must seek a way to prove her right to her family's wealth, to defeat her enemy, and more than anything, to stay alive.

The Grandmaster
Unrelated strangers are being murdered in a brutal fashion. Now it's up to crime-scene cleaner Mike Chambers, with the help of the police, in the form of his friend, DC James Worth, to track down the killer and stop the trail of carnage.

Lunch Hour
One office. Many lives. It is that time of day: the time for poorly-filled, pre-packaged sandwiches; the time to run errands you won't have enough time for; the time to fall in love, to kill or be killed, to take advice from an alien. It's the Lunch Hour.

Made in the USA
Charleston, SC
12 August 2014